SOLEIL

A Mustang's Story

To: Rachel

Best Wishes

Enjoy

Lisa Holderby

SOLEIL

A Mustang's Story

Written by
Lisa Holderby

Illustrations by
Sheila Walker

This book is dedicated to all of the
little girls who dream of wild horses,
and especially to the little girl
in my life, my daughter, Anissa.

Introduction

oleil, *A Mustang's Story* is based on many true events in the life of a wild mustang filly. Soleil once ran free in Wyoming, roaming the countryside with a herd of wild horses. The filly was captured and placed in the government's mustang adoption program in February 2005 as a result of the Bureau of Land Management's round up. Wild horses are offered for adoption because there is not enough land to sustain them for survival in the wild.

Mustangs are legendary horses and a symbol of America's national identity. Just like the bald eagle, they should be protected and preserved. These mustangs deserve our respect, love, and care.

This book tells their story. I also hope it helps in finding homes or sponsors for the hundreds of wild mustangs in need.

I adopted Soleil via the Internet in March 2005. *Soleil, A Mustang's Story* is a work of fiction based on facts. My life has never been the same since adopting her!

–Lisa Holderby

Contents

Chapter One

The Capture

The morning light rose over the mountains and fresh dew glistened on the high meadow. Crisp Wyoming air swirled over tall evergreen trees that surrounded a group of wild horses. A beautiful little filly with a flaxen mane raced across the misty field. The little filly's mother, the head mare, watched intently. She was making sure that her little one did not wander far from the herd.

The flaxen mane filly loved running with the herd. At times she ran so fast that the other yearlings could not catch up with her.

This morning the herd was at their favorite watering spot where the spring was sweet and cool. The little filly raced faster and farther across the open land until she almost lost sight of the herd.

The herd's stallion, her father, paced back and forth. His ears flicked forward as he stood protectively over the rest of the herd. The filly's mother neighed for her to come back, warning her not to go any farther. Her mother knew there were dangers in the mountains—mountain lions, wolves, and man.

How could anything ever hurt or catch me? thought the little filly. *I'm so fast.* The wildflowers burst open with colors of purple and yellow, while new green leaves on the white-barked aspens swayed to the morning breeze.

The past winter had been hard for the wild horses. The herd had constantly moved from one place to the next, trying to find food and shelter from the bitter cold of the Rocky Mountains. Today was different from past winter days. The little filly could feel the warmth on her back.

Racing ahead of the other horses again, she ran farther from the herd. Urgently, her mother warned her with very loud neighs to come back. The mare sensed something was wrong. It was too silent in the surrounding woods. The other horses moved restlessly among each other, also sensing danger.

Roar! Suddenly a sound came from the mountains. Something the little filly had never seen before appeared above her. The shiny machine hovered and glistened in the sunlight. On the other side of the mountain wild mustangs were being rounded up with a second strange object. Both of these things were moving all of the herds in one direction.

The filly bounded away from the terrifying object. But was still not fast enough to keep up with the older horses and she watched as they left her behind. She cried out, *Wait for me! I can't run any faster.*

The filly's heart pounded from exhaustion and fear as she saw her mother lead the herd, screaming for her to catch up. The filly neighed as loudly as she could. *Don't leave me!*

The dust from the flying machine blinded her. Its sound hurt her ears and now she could no longer see or hear any of the other horses. The gleaming machine chased the herd away from the mountains and the loud noise drove her deeper into the woods. She stumbled and fell, trying to escape, trying to neigh, but only silent air escaped her mouth. For the first time, the little filly found herself alone and frightened. Her small hooves were broken and sore from the rocks and stones. She neighed once more in desperation, but it was no use. The other horses were gone.

This machine that had chased her was a helicopter. She had never seen anything like it. She shook from fear and exhaustion while trying to get up. She was down and more vulnerable, so she struggled to her feet. *Help! Please come back for me!* She screamed, but her cries could not be heard over the helicopter's noise.

Men on horseback drove the filly and other horses toward a corral. Frightened and shaken from her fall, she was unaware that she had been locked up and could not escape the corral. She wandered aimlessly through the new herd.

The little filly was very scared. She did not understand that she had been caught up in a routine government roundup that thinned out the wild mustang herds. The little filly didn't know that there was no longer enough land to support the size of the herds. The wild horses were to be put up for adoption to the public. The unlucky ones that would not get adopted could possibly be sold and killed.

She roamed around the large corral and felt saddened from her capture and confinement. She could not escape the 6-foot high enclosure that separated her from freedom.

Where am I? she thought.

With her head hung low, she watched while other horses were being tagged and freeze-branded on the side of the neck. Branding the wild mustangs was how the Bureau of Land Management numbered the horses and kept track of the adopted ones.

Some horses were taken out and never returned. Others, like the little filly, remained in the holding pen. She watched while some of the horses tried to climb the fencing that held them captive.

The little filly stayed at this facility for several weeks. There was no way to escape. She would never see her mother or the herd again.

Chapter Two

Man

She was the smallest filly in the pen. The older and bigger horses shoved and bullied her—biting, kicking, and chasing her from her food. She was always the last one to eat and became very thin. The little filly was low in the pecking order because of her size and age.

One morning a cowboy entered the pen. His voice sounded very gruff and mean. "Get in," he yelled tossing a lead rope over her head and leading her to a trailer. "Go on!" Once inside, she was afraid of being trampled on because the trailer was overcrowded.

There was not enough room in the large trailer for all of the horses, but what alarmed her more than the fear of being trampled was that she was leaving the only place she had ever known. *If only I could escape*, she thought, *and then I could find my way back home.*

Finally, they arrived at another facility

where more wild horses were held.

She trembled as a man came to inspect her. His hat made her feel uneasy. He was speaking to the other men at the facility. She wanted to bolt. Their body motions told it all—the eye contact, the pointing and waving of a white flag to make her run in circles. She was the center of attention, and that frightened her more than anything. *Please help me. I am afraid of man.* she neighed out to the other horses, but they ignored her cries.

The filly was afraid of man, and for good reason. The man looked her over closely, and put her in a narrow metal cage called a chute. The filly felt trapped and confined in this small space.

"Hey, girl! Let me put this halter on you," the man said to her. The strange, uncomfortable leather piece was placed over her head.

She rubbed her head against the railing trying to scrape the halter off. She saw bridles and saddles put on some horses, and to her amazement, the horses tolerated it. *No way!* she thought, fearing the day man would try to place a saddle or bridle on her.

Most shocking though, was when the little filly watched other horses being ridden. *I'll never let anybody ride me!* she promised herself.

The next day the same man came back and singled her out from the other horses.

"Eee-hahh, this way," he shouted and taunted, lunging toward her as he put her into another horse trailer. This time she was alone. There was fresh hay and water in the trailer, and soon she had eaten until she was full. She realized how tired she was and dozed off to the sounds of a humming engine. *Will I ever see my home again?* she thought just before she fell asleep. She slept standing, as many horses do. She could not risk lying down.

She catnapped, peeking glimpses of the changing terrain. She looked through the trailer bars and saw her new surroundings. It was very different from the high meadow. *Where can I be now?* she thought worriedly. The land was very flat with a few rolling hills, but the smells that filled her quivering nostrils were delicious, and the flaxen mane filly was eager to get out. The freshly cut pastures with pleasant scents reminded her that she was hungry.

Finally, the trailer slowly came to a stop in front of a huge barn. The door opened and the gruff man motioned for her. She stood in the corner of the trailer, afraid to move.

"Come on, get out," he said as he pulled on her lead rope. She was forced out and into a round corral. Once again she was frightened. There were a few other men around the corral too. Inside the corral, she started to run and snort at the people surrounding her.

Still tired, she managed to proudly trot around the corral. One of the men who had been watching came into the corral and started chasing her, making her change directions and stopping her for only a moment.

The filly kicked up her heels at the man and snorted, running in circles at the people who stared at her from the fence. The man pressed the filly to run again in a circle and moved her from one end of the corral to the other. They played this game for hours. The trip had been exhausting enough and now this man chasing her was more than she could handle.

She stopped, her nostrils flared. She noticed a woman sitting on the grass outside the corral. The woman's hair was the same gold color as her own mane. The woman never took her eyes off the filly as the horse raced around the corral. She locked eyes once again with the woman on the ground. She sensed something about the woman—a kindness—and at that moment, she just gave up fighting. She stood quietly while the woman walked slowly toward her. Her hand reached out through the fence and touched her ever so lightly on the nose.

"Easy girl," the man said softly. The woman watched and stood as the man spoke little words of encouragement. "No one is going to hurt you," he said kindly. When the man rubbed her neck, the filly quivered at his touch. He slowly moved his hand up and rubbed the soft end of her nose.

"Elizabeth," the man called to the woman nearby, "come on in and say hello." The woman walked slowly into the corral and held out her hand for the little filly to smell.

It would be a smell that the filly would never forget. The woman stroked the horse's mane and neck and said, "I will never hurt you. You are safe now…" The words were soft and quiet. The filly dropped her ear closer to hear as Elizabeth whispered, " … my beautiful girl."

The filly closed her eyes and dropped her head, letting out a huge sigh.

Chapter Three

A New Home

In the wild, the mustang herd had always faced a food shortage, especially in the winter. Wild horses had to be smart and remember where their food and watering spots were. There was no shelter from the blistering wind, so the herd clumped together for warmth. Some days the herd had to search miles for a small piece of ice to quench their thirst.

Now, Elizabeth took care of the filly at home, making sure she had food, water, and shelter. She piled the hayloft full of hay and grain to feed the filly. She fed her twice daily to add weight to the horse. Elizabeth was relieved to finally have the filly at home. What was she going to name her? Her mane was so full and bright, that it shined like the sun. She found it hard to believe this beautiful animal had been running free just a couple of months ago. Her beauty took Elizabeth's breath away; she could only stare at the filly trying to picture what it must have been like, being captured.

Satisfied now, in her new pasture, the filly kicked up and ran from one end to the other. There were some things about her new home that the mustang did not like, though. Even though the barn was warm with wide windows, the filly didn't like staying in it. The little filly thought, *I don't want to be closed in.*

Next door to her paddock was a gelding named Cheyenne who greeted her with happy neighs on the first day. But the filly saw him wearing a bridle and saddle, causing her to run to the far side of the pasture. *No way will I wear those!* she thought.

Slowly, she began to feel comfortable and safe in her new home, especially after Elizabeth walked the whole pasture with her. She showed the filly where everything was, including her watering trough and feed bucket.

The next morning, Elizabeth introduced her to Cheyenne through the fence. They sniffed each other and rubbed noses. The filly remembered the other horses from her herd and was glad to have a friend. Without his bridle and halter Cheyenne didn't frighten her at all. *I have a friend next door,* thought the filly, *and plenty of green grass, too!*

Each day, the filly looked forward to Elizabeth's visit. She would patiently wait for Elizabeth to return because of all the treats and kisses that came with each visit.

"I finally have a name for you," said Elizabeth one day while she brushed the filly's coat. As if she understood the words, the filly turned her head and looked directly into Elizabeth's eyes. "Soleil," Elizabeth whispered, "because you have brought sunshine into my life and have made me happier than you could ever know." Elizabeth thought of her own losses, the death of her old horse and not having any children. She shook her head in disbelief, holding on to Soleil. She had dreamt of wild horses since her childhood, and now she had one. She smiled at Soleil and hugged her a little more tightly.

That evening, after Soleil was fed, Elizabeth sat down in the pasture with Soleil standing next to her. Soleil felt so comfortable that she laid down, with Elizabeth sitting next to her. Elizabeth sat back next to Soleil and gazed up at the stars. Listening to Soleil sleep, she watched her chest rise and fall with each breath. Elizabeth still couldn't believe she was lying next to a horse that was once wild.

"Since you like people so much now, I'll take you to meet the neighbors next door soon," Elizabeth said. Soleil woke to the sound of Elizabeth's voice and lifted her head as if to say, *Okay!*

Soleil had seen these people from a distance.

Elizabeth suddenly touched Soleil's neck where she was freeze branded and ran her fingers very slowly across the mark from end to end. "Did it hurt you, girl?" Elizabeth asked her tenderly.

"Someday, I'll take you back to your home in the high meadow," Elizabeth promised. "You can visit your old friends."

Soleil ran to Elizabeth whenever she whistled for her. It became her calling card for treats. Every afternoon, Elizabeth called Soleil while standing on the top part of the pasture and watched her gallop up the hill.

Soleil had grown a lot over the summer and had started to fill out. She was starting to look like a horse—no longer a filly. Soleil's favorite past time was stretching out in the pasture and soaking up the sun.

If Elizabeth couldn't see her, she got worried and ran down to the pasture to make sure Soleil was okay. Soleil just lifted her head and looked at Elizabeth and thought, *Don't get too worked up lady, I'm only sunbathing!* Soleil's name suited her well, from her rich red coat to her golden mane that sparkled in the bright daylight. Elizabeth would call her, "Sun girl," as she gently patted Soleil's nose.

Almost every day Elizabeth walked the pasture with Soleil, teaching her to walk on lead. The halter was the only device Soleil could tolerate. Whenever Soleil saw a bridle in Elizabeth's hands or a saddle over the corral, she ran to the other side of the pen and neighed, *No way, not even for a treat!* Elizabeth was very patient with her.

Most days they would see their neighbors from a distance. Mr. and Mrs. Adkins and their ten-year old niece—who lived on the farm next door—usually stood on the hill and waved to them.

"We'll go visit soon," Elizabeth promised.. Little did she know that the meeting wouldn't happen the way Elizabeth had planned.

Chapter Four

The Girl Next Door

Spring turned into summer, and summer rolled into fall. The leaves on the maple and oak trees turned into a vibrant mixture of gold, red, and orange. Soleil's formal training had started and she had just returned from a training facility. There she had learned good manners and how to back up, stand still, load properly in a trailer, and work on a lunge line.

One morning Elizabeth worked her on a lunge line, which teaches a horse to walk, trot, and canter with verbal commands. Soleil was very smart, as all mustangs are. She reared up in front of Elizabeth. She didn't want to work anymore. Elizabeth immediately reprimanded her by jerking on her lunge chain. Rearing would not be tolerated. After their morning training, Soleil calmed down.

Elizabeth brushed all of the night's tangles and burrs out of her curly, golden mane.

Soleil moved her rear around so Elizabeth could massage her muscles.

Soleil loved to be groomed and Elizabeth always knew the right spots to brush and scratch. After grooming, she patiently waited for her beloved treat—molasses and oat muffins.

Even with all the comforts Elizabeth provided, it was hard for Soleil to realize that there would be a reliable food source for the up- and-coming winter. Her internal clock told her that winter was approaching. The days were getting shorter, and her coat had begun to lengthen to prepare itself for the harsh, cold season. She also felt the urge to eat more to sustain her through the food shortage that had happened in the wild. "Soleil, you are such a chow hound," Elizabeth laughed at her.

Soleil was grazing in the pasture. It was a very windy day, and Elizabeth was cleaning out the tack room. The trees swayed like music in the wind. A lonesome leaf rolled across the pasture, a sure sign of the coming of winter.

Soleil noticed one of their neighbors

standing on the far side of the pasture. It was the small girl with long dark hair. She was alone and looking down at Soleil from the top of the pasture. Soleil heard a muffled cry and low sobs. Soleil lifted her head and walked toward the small girl who now sat near an old oak tree. As Soleil approached, she could see the little girl's face. It was streaked with tears.

Soleil dropped her muzzle down to sniff the child. She brushed her soft whiskers over the tear-stained hands and face. The little girl reached up to pat Soleil's nose. She stopped crying at that moment, and her sparkling big brown eyes looked into Soleil's. Soleil nuzzled harder, and a slight smile came across the girl's face. She let the girl play with her mane.

"Well, you finally met Emily!" Elizabeth's voice startled both of them. The little girl wiped her face as Elizabeth drew closer.

"Emily, this is Soleil," Elizabeth said. "And Soleil, this is Emily, who lives next door." Just then Emily's aunt Jenny walked down from their farm. "Emily, it's time for you to come in," she said trying to take Emily's hand. Emily brushed her away and went around to hug Soleil.

"I will, Aunt Jenny," she mumbled turning her back to her aunt.

"Jenny, I'm so glad Soleil finally met you and Emily. I was going take her over after a few more training lessons," Elizabeth said.

"We wanted to meet her too. What a pretty girl," Mrs. Adkins said as she walked up and placed her hand on Soleil's neck. "What do you think, Emily?" Emily smiled at Soleil.

"She really is a sweet horse," Emily said hugging Soleil warmly. Mrs. Adkins and Elizabeth shared a knowing look.

"Emily, you can drop by at the barn anytime and visit Soleil and Cheyenne after school, if Aunt Jenny says it's okay, of course," Elizabeth said, winking at Mrs. Adkins who shook her head in agreement.

"Thank you, Elizabeth," Emily said. "I would like to do that."

"Okay, see you soon, then," Elizabeth said as she took Soleil by the halter and led her home.

Soleil and Elizabeth walked down the hill toward the barn.

Soleil looked back at Emily one more time as she walked back to the barn.

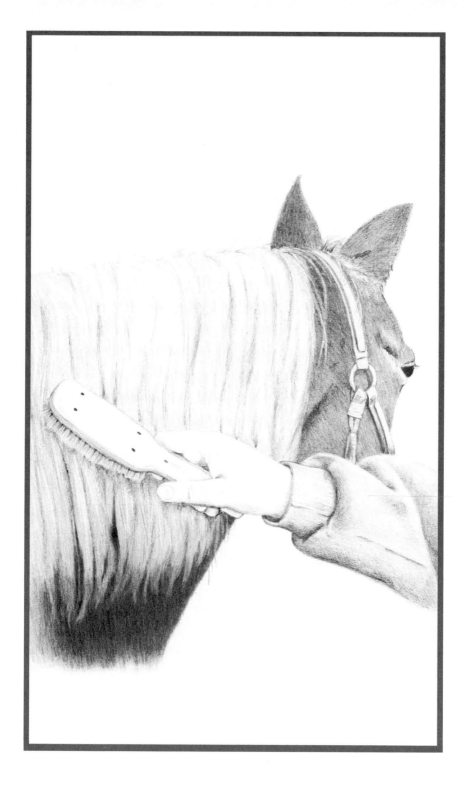

Chapter Five

A Sense of Trust

After Emily's formal introduction, Elizabeth trained and groomed Soleil on a daily basis, but Emily never stopped by. Soleil did not see Emily for several days, either. She often looked up the hill by the old oak tree to see if she was there.

Finally, one afternoon, Soleil saw Emily on top of the hill. She raced eagerly to the hilltop to greet her.

"Soleil!" Emily shouted, a smile spreading across her face. Emily held out her hand, and to Soleil's surprise a shiny red apple sat there for her.

"This is for you," Emily said, offering her the sweet treat. Soleil gently took the apple from Emily's hand. "You really like that, don't you, girl?" Emily giggled. The two of them spent the rest of the afternoon together chasing each other and playing in the pasture like best friends.

From then on, this became a ritual between them in the afternoons.

"Let's keep this our secret," Emily said shyly. "We wouldn't want to make Elizabeth jealous." Soleil neighed as if in agreement. During every visit, Soleil heard Emily crying when she had to leave to go home. Soleil still wondered why the girl was so unhappy.

One evening while Elizabeth was training Soleil, they heard Mrs. Adkins shouting. "Emily, come back home now!" she hollered.

Emily darted out the door slamming it with a bang. The girl ran into the pasture and up to Soleil, wrapping her arms around the horse's neck. She buried her face into Soleil's mane and let out the most painful sound Elizabeth had ever heard. Emily was crying so hard she could barely breathe. Her tears wet Soleil's mane and her arms trembled.

Elizabeth put her arm around Emily's shoulders and said, "Emily, it's okay, don't cry."

Emily fell down around Soleil's legs. "Where are my parents? Why did they leave me? And my aunt's always angry at me for something."

Elizabeth held her. "Hush now, Emily, your Aunt Jenny and Uncle Phil love you very much. They'll take good care of you.

Soleil and I love you and think you are very special."

That day, Elizabeth and Soleil learned that Emily was an orphan, and that the Adkins, her Aunt Jenny and Uncle Phil, had adopted her after her parents had died in a car accident.

Soleil liked this little girl very much and felt her pain. She was an orphan too, taken away from what she had loved and known best. She had been brought to live in another home too—luckily it was a wonderful home. But she still sometimes wondered about her family and the herd.

Elizabeth talked to Emily and held her. Emily looked up at Elizabeth and said, "Do you think Soleil is sad that she doesn't have *her* parents anymore?" She asked.

"I suppose she misses them, but she has a new and safe home like you do," Elizabeth answered. "It's normal to miss your parents and be sad. Just keep them in your heart and they will never be gone." Emily smiled at Elizabeth and patted Soleil's legs. Soleil looked down at her and nuzzled her face.

I remember being left behind, Soleil thought, understanding just how sad Emily was.

After their talk, Elizabeth took Emily back

home to her Aunt Jenny.

"Hi Jenny, Emily feels much better now. Don't you, honey?" Elizabeth said reassuringly.

"I'll be okay," Emily said bravely as Aunt Jenny gave her a loving hug.

Elizabeth, Emily, and Mrs. Adkins went inside for a little while to have some cocoa and cookies while Soleil waited outside at the pasture fence.

After that incident, Emily and Soleil trusted each other and were great friends. Many afternoons passed between the two of them.

Winter months soon came along, and the pasture took on the look of a frosted wonderland. Snow was heaped on the barn roof and glistened on the bare trees. Icicles hung from the western side of the barn. Soleil realized, to her delight, that the food kept coming, even if there wasn't any more grass to graze upon. Elizabeth had purchased a hay feeder so that Soleil had full access to it day and night. Elizabeth was hoping one day to get another horse to share the hay feeder with Soleil.

Still Elizabeth never stalled Soleil into the barn except to feed her. Otherwise, Soleil could come and go as she pleased. Soleil sensed that Elizabeth understood that she liked being outside and free.

Her coat was full and thick again, and she looked more like a woolly mammoth than a horse. On the warm days, Soleil would catch some of the sun's warm rays and curl up, much like a napping dog. Soleil didn't see much of Emily because of the snow and cold weather, but whenever Emily did come to visit in the pasture, she didn't cry anymore. A sense of trust bonded them, and their interactions were very special. Soleil enjoyed the closeness they shared.

Today, Elizabeth came to the pasture in the afternoon and saw Emily with Soleil. Elizabeth stood on the hill and peered down at the two of them watching for some time, and then she realized that Emily must have been visiting Soleil secretly. "Well, what do you know," Elizabeth thought as she watched Emily brush Soleil's tail. Elizabeth noticed how different Emily was—clearly happier than a few months ago. Spending time with Soleil seemed to have helped her.

She wondered what it must have been like for Emily to lose her parents and also how Soleil felt being captured. Those thoughts saddened Elizabeth as she watched the two of them together, both orphaned. A trust bonded them together, because they each had a similar loss that the other one could relate to.

Looking up to see Elizabeth, Soleil nickered, *Hello.*

"Hey, you two," Elizabeth called out, "you are having too much fun without me!" She looked at Emily and added, "Have you gotten her bridle on her yet?"

"Emily have you been keeping this a secret? These afternoon visits!"

"No, we're just hanging out," Emily said quietly, looking down toward the ground.

"I can see that," Elizabeth joked. "It's great to see you with Soleil, she loves your company, and I really could use some help with her, you know …."

"You really mean it, Elizabeth?" Emily asked.

"Yes, I do—especially about the bridle and stuff," she said. "Soleil's still giving me a hard time with that. She's so stubborn!"

"She just needs time," Emily said while hugging Soleil's neck.

Chapter Six

Partners

"Morning, Elizabeth," said Mrs. Adkins as she opened the door and peered out.

"Hi, Jenny," Elizabeth replied. "I'm here to ask if Emily can help get Soleil ready for an upcoming article a local newspaper is doing about Soleil and the wild mustangs."

"Sure, I think Emily would love that!" Mrs. Adkins said warmly. "Emily is so much happier since she met Soleil. Phil and I are thinking about getting her a horse of her own," she added. "It's helped her deal with losing her parents."

"I know," said Elizabeth. "I think that would be great for her too, and …"

"Are you talking about me?" Emily asked, suddenly appearing at the front door.

"Yes," Mrs. Adkins laughed. "Elizabeth is here to ask if you would be interested in helping her with Soleil after school and on the weekends. She is getting her ready for an interview about the wild mustangs."

Emily grinned from ear to ear and yelped, "Yes, yes, can I, Aunt Jenny?" Soleil watched while Emily jumped up and down in happiness. Aunt Jenny obviously said yes.

Soleil started running and bucking at that moment, clearly having a good time. Elizabeth, Emily, and Mrs. Adkins starting laughing, and Elizabeth said, "Emily, your excitement is contagious. Just look at Soleil!"

The next day after school Emily came down to the pasture to start working with Elizabeth. "Let's clean the barn first," said Elizabeth as they both grabbed shovels and rakes and began working together. Soleil watched. From time to time Emily would turn and give Soleil a big smile and pat. Soleil would nudge Emily along with her nose, making Emily giggle.

Elizabeth's heart skipped a beat when she saw the two of them, happy that this girl had bonded with her horse.

Elizabeth purchased a mounting block so Emily could stand and brush Soleil's mane, also thinking that perhaps one day it would help her be able to mount Soleil.

Of course, no one had ridden Soleil yet. Elizabeth and Emily were still trying to coax her to wear a bridle and bit, which took a lot of teamwork. They couldn't saddle her without Soleil kicking and bucking—they just couldn't get the gear near her, no matter what.

Amazingly though, Soleil would stand very still for Emily to groom and pet her. "Here's how you can braid Soleil's mane," Elizabeth showed Emily. The two of them stood on either end of her, braiding and twisting her mane. Soleil loved the attention they gave her.

Most of winter passed this way, because the pasture was too icy for much training. Whenever they could, they worked on getting Soleil used to wearing a bridle and bit.

During all this time, Emily was talking more and more to Elizabeth, telling her about the tragic death of her parents and about what it was like living with her mother's sister, Aunt Jenny and her husband Uncle Phil. Elizabeth wouldn't say much, she'd just listen and give Emily a hug. She was glad Emily was adjusting the best she could.

"Emily, it's time to really start getting ready for that interview. It's next Saturday," Elizabeth said one evening at the barn. Emily leaped with joy when Elizabeth told her the reporter would be at the farm early to shoot pictures of Soleil. They talked about how important it would be to tell about the wild mustangs and the BLM's adoption program.

"Aunt Jenny already said you could stay over at my house the night before so we can get an extra early start preparing Soleil for her interview and photos," said Elizabeth.

"I can't wait," exclaimed Emily, jumping up and down happily. Soleil was so excited that she began to run with Emily, bucking and kicking up her heels.

"We really are partners, aren't we"? Emily asked that evening with brown eyes as big as saucers and a huge smile. Elizabeth smiled too, and took Emily's hand. The three of them walked up the hill to get ready for the weekend. Soleil stood and watched through the fence as Emily and Elizabeth disappeared to separate homes.

Chapter Seven

The Article

The days were getting longer now, and spring was just around the corner. All of the snow had disappeared and new buds were appearing on the barren limbs of the trees. There was fresh new grass appearing in the pasture, and Soleil noticed the birds were beginning to return to the pasture. Geese often accompanied her in the pasture on their migration route south.

Elizabeth and Emily were in the barn preparing a bath for Soleil. She could smell the sudsy aroma of the shampoo that Emily was mixing in the tack room.

I hope this bath is not for me, Soleil thought. The newspaper reporter would be there too early for them to wash her in the morning. Elizabeth decided that it was warm enough now to bathe the horse. They would put her in the stall that night to keep her from rolling.

Soleil had never stayed shut up in the stall

overnight before. So Elizabeth and Emily had taken turns getting her inside the barn with feed, and then shutting her up for small periods of time.

At first Soleil panicked when Elizabeth shut the door. The horse started prancing around nervously. Then Emily came up to her and said, "I promise you, girl, it will not harm you."

Emily even got into the stall with Soleil. Soleil watched the small girl with curiosity while Emily walked from one corner of the stall to the next, talking to her the whole time. "Look, Soleil, you can see Cheyenne from your window," Emily pointed out.

This is not so bad, I can see out without being outside, Soleil thought.

Now, the night before the big interview, she'd have to stay in the stall. Elizabeth and Emily continued with their preparations.

"Soleil, you need to be real pretty for the pictures tomorrow," Emily said softly.

When Elizabeth grabbed her lead rope,

Soleil started to make a dash for it, but Elizabeth was too fast. Emily quieted her while Elizabeth sponged her down with warm soapy water.

"That a girl," Emily said softly as they scrubbed the winter's dirt away.

"Hey, Elizabeth, look at Soleil!" Emily shouted, laughing. Soleil had no idea that she was wearing a Mohawk that Emily had designed with her soapy mane

Soleil was pretty quiet through the whole process until Elizabeth tried to wash the soap out of her tail. Then she ran in circles while Elizabeth held on to her tail! The hose spitting out water frightened Soleil. Emily was on the ground laughing hysterically watching the two of them. Soleil had tucked her tail with Elizabeth hanging on behind her, soaked to the skin.

"Hey, Elizabeth why don't you just soak her tail in a bucket with some clean water?" Emily suggested. Elizabeth said, "Now you're thinking." Elizabeth and Emily took towels and rubbed her down.

Soleil relaxed and gave in to the attention.

"Liz what exactly will the article be about? I mean, will they tell the story about the helicopters rounding them up?" Emily asked curiously while they rubbed down Soleil.

"Emily, I hope the article tells the whole story about what happens to the ones that don't get adopted—the ones who are not as fortunate as Soleil," Elizabeth answered.

"Liz, can they really die?" asked Emily. Elizabeth lowered her head and sadly nodded yes.

Soleil turned her head to Elizabeth. She knew what happened to them. If only she could speak. *I'll tell you what happened,* she neighed as she looked at Elizabeth. It was a saddened look that Elizabeth turned away from.

After they dried her, shined up her coat and detangled her mane, Elizabeth told Emily to put Soleil in the barn so she wouldn't get dirty before the morning. Soleil instantly neighed for them to come back.

"You'll be okay tonight, girl," said Emily, running back to her.

The next morning, at dawn, the sun was just rising over the east side of the pasture as Emily and Elizabeth ran down to the barn to let Soleil out. Emily was so impressed that Soleil hadn't messed in her stall.

"Good, girl," she praised her. A little while later, Soleil was eating her soaked sugar beet pulp when she heard an unfamiliar voice from outside the barn. She raised her head.

A woman was walking down the pasture with her notebook in hand. "Good Morning," she called out. "You must be Elizabeth!"

"What is it like owning a wild horse?" the reporter, who had just arrived with her crew, asked Elizabeth.

"It's very special," Elizabeth answered, going into the barn and taking Soleil outside by her lead rope and halter.

"How so?" The reporter wanted to know.

"You have to win their trust," Elizabeth answered as she looked directly at Soleil. Elizabeth introduced Soleil and Emily, and then told the story about how she had adopted Soleil through the Internet adoption program. "The mustangs are running out of land. The range is getting too small to support the herds," she went on. "Preserving and protecting the wild mustangs is just as important as preserving our land. They are part of our American heritage." Elizabeth also talked to the reporter about the mustang's intelligence and athletic ability.

"What have you learned from this experience?" asked the reporter.

"I've learned more about myself from Soleil than anything or anyone has ever taught me.

She keeps me real," Elizabeth calmly answered while stroking Soleil's back. "I had to learn to be patient," Elizabeth said. "Patience was not one of my strong points."

Emily beamed when Elizabeth spoke about how she helped with Soleil's care and how gently Soleil behaved around Emily.

"Soleil," called Emily. As Soleil walked gingerly to Emily, Emily did figure eights underneath Soleil's legs to show the reporter just how gentle the horse was. The reporter had a photographer take lots of photos as the reporter wrote a mile a minute, taking notes on everything Elizabeth talked about, from how the mustangs lived in the wild to how they were captured and put up for adoption.

Soleil posed for every shot, enjoying all the attention.

"I don't think I have ever met a horse who enjoys having her picture taken as much as Soleil." The reporter laughed. So did Elizabeth and Emily.

The reporter told them that the article would be in the next issue of the local horse paper. Emily couldn't wait to see what the reporter wrote about Soleil and the wild mustangs.

After the reporter left, Emily and Elizabeth stayed in the pasture for a while talking about how well it went and just chatting. Soleil started to graze, listening to them.

"How is everything going, Emily?" Elizabeth asked.

"Better now. I guess," she said, thinking carefully as she spoke. "I'm a lot happier than I was, Elizabeth. Thanks for letting me help with Soleil. I really love her—I wish I had a horse of my own," she sighed.

"Maybe someday you will have one as special as Soleil," Elizabeth offered.

"I feel better about staying with Aunt Jenny and Uncle Phil now, too," Emily said after a few moments. Elizabeth was glad that she and Soleil could help Emily feel better. She wondered when Mrs. Adkins would share the good news to Emily about getting her own horse. What a surprise that would be!

Emily hugged Elizabeth who wrapped her arms around the girl and just held her.

The three of them spent most of the day in the pasture, until in the early evening Emily waved good-bye as she headed home with her long hair flowing behind her.

Chapter Eight
The Ride

pring had finally arrived. Soleil was now a two-year-old. After months of gentle persuasion, Elizabeth and Emily had enticed her into wearing a bridle and to accept the bit in her mouth, yet she still was reluctant have a saddle put on her. Elizabeth kept trying whenever she could, since Soleil was now almost big enough to be ridden, but Soleil would not give in. No way, she'd say to herself whenever Elizabeth brought the saddle out. She had vowed a long time ago that man would never ride her. She was a wild mustang, not a domesticated horse.

Although she loved and trusted Elizabeth and let her put a bridle on and a bit into her mouth, a saddle was different somehow; it was too confining and uncomfortable. Elizabeth could lay the blanket on her back and even position the saddle for short amounts of time, but the moment Elizabeth would reach for the girth, Soleil pinned her ears back with a threatening look. When Elizabeth tried to tighten the girth, Soleil lifted a hind leg as if she would kick. She hated the saddle.

Don't put that on me, Soleil thought fiercely. Elizabeth would get firm with her when she acted like this, but Soleil would not submit to the girth.

Emily never tried to push Soleil's limits. She was always just happy walking with her or lying down next to her in the pasture.

Elizabeth's training of Soleil had become more intense, teaching her groundwork, like backing and stopping with the, "Whoa," command. She had even started pulling sideways on the bit, which Soleil had found to be very annoying. Elizabeth was trying to teach to her to give in to the bit. Soleil was a quick learner and picked up very easily on these lessons, but she just wasn't going to stand still while Elizabeth tried to tighten the girth or mount her—not even when she used the mounting block for leverage.

Sometimes Emily would watch while Elizabeth tried to swing her legs over her back, Soleil sidestepping every time. Emily giggled as she watched. "Why do you want to ride her so bad?" Emily asked.

"Because I've dreamed of riding her and have waited patiently for this day" was the answer.

"Elizabeth really doesn't get it, does she girl?" Emily would just sigh and say to Soleil. Elizabeth explained to Emily that she didn't want to force Soleil to be ridden, but she was old enough and big enough now for Elizabeth to ride her.

Soleil had exceeded the usual size of a mustang and had really put on great deal of muscle. Her legs were thick and powerful and her chest was full and broad. The year had done wonders for her size and her coat. It now glistened with a reddish tone. The Bureau of Land Management had her listed a sorrel on the paperwork, but she really was a red-roan; the white hairs had blended with the coppery red ones. Her mane was still as blonde as ever. Elizabeth was proud of her and looked forward to the day when they could ride together.

For the better part of the spring, Elizabeth and Soleil continued to butt heads about whether or not Soleil would allow her to tighten the girth. But Elizabeth finally got the girth tightened. It was a real victory, but a small one.

Once, Soleil let Elizabeth climb onto her back—just to buck her off. Soleil didn't want any stuff on her. She loved Elizabeth, but never forgot the cowboys who rounded her up and how mechanical and unhappy their horses seemed.

That afternoon, Emily and Soleil were just hanging out in the pasture. Emily was studying the problem with Soleil's behavior of being ridden. "I know why you don't want anyone to ride you girl."

"I understand," Emily said quietly. Soleil just let out a sigh. She was just misunderstood by Elizabeth.

Emily reached up and patted Soleil's back. "It's okay to be ridden," Emily said with the sweetest tone. Emily stroked her neck and hugged her. Then she went into the tack room and pulled out her mounting block. Emily knew how important it was for Elizabeth to ride Soleil. Elizabeth said to Emily more than once "I used to dream of riding wild horses."

She brought it over to Soleil and climbed up, and before Soleil knew Emily had jumped on her back, she froze.

Emily reached down and hugged her neck and said, "That's not so bad is it?" Emily said reaching down and hugging her neck.

Soleil took one step and then another, before long she and Emily were walking in circles. There weren't any bits, saddles or bridles on her, just one young girl with a handful of mane.

Emily, satisfied with her accomplishment, rolled off and went to give Soleil some of her favorite treats. Soleil followed Emily to the end of the pasture. "Elizabeth will be so pleased with us," Emily said.

Chapter Nine

The Surprise

Emily and Soleil kept this secret between the two of them for a while. Elizabeth did not have a clue that Emily had ridden Soleil bareback. She was still working Soleil in the mornings on the lunge line and rarely tried to ride her.

Late on a summer afternoon, the weather was extremely humid and hot. Elizabeth, Emily, and Soleil were listening to music. Elizabeth was singing to Soleil "Wild Horses" at the top of her lungs. Emily couldn't contain her secret any longer to Elizabeth.

"Why don't you just ride her bareback?" Emily asked casually.

Elizabeth just stared at Emily puzzled.

"How can I ride her bareback?" asked Elizabeth. "I can't even get the saddle on her."

"Maybe she just doesn't like the saddle and girth," Emily said quickly.

Elizabeth shrugged and rolled her eyes as

Emily pulled at Elizabeth's arms. "Come on, try it," the young girl coaxed.

Soleil was grazing when Elizabeth walked up to her. She rubbed Soleil's nose and kissed her eyes looking over at Emily.

"Here goes," she said. Swiftly Elizabeth hoisted herself on top of Soleil's back.

Soleil froze. She turned her head to see Elizabeth and thought, *Now you finally get it!*

Elizabeth was stunned and thrilled at the same time. Soleil began walking around the pasture as if they had done this a hundred times.

Emily was laughing and smiling at Elizabeth. "She didn't like the saddle!" Emily shouted.

"You knew this would work! How... when did you figure this out?" Elizabeth asked.

Emily told Elizabeth about her ride, too, and they cheered with happiness.

Elizabeth was finally riding her horse—the one she had dreamed of from the first time she saw Soleil's picture on the Internet. She had waited a long time for this day, and it had been so simple.

Everyone was happy. Soleil was relieved that the tension was over with Elizabeth, and

Emily was so thrilled that Elizabeth finally rode Soleil. Emily said "I can't wait to tell Aunt Jenny and Uncle Phil what we did today. It was a great day!"

"Yes, it was!" Elizabeth yelled at the top of her lungs. Emily wasn't sure who was the happiest of the three of them. Then Emily heard her aunt call her for dinner and ran up the hill waving good-bye to Soleil and Elizabeth.

Elizabeth called out, "Hey wait for me. I was invited too!"

In Emily's haste she had forgotten that Elizabeth was having dinner with them this evening. Elizabeth called out, "You go on. I need to get washed up before dinner. I won't be long." Soleil watched Emily run up the hill toward her home. Elizabeth walked up to her and lifted her head and looked into her eyes and said, "You just made one little girl's life-long dream come true—**mine!**"

Soleil turned toward Elizabeth and let out a soft nicker, which meant, *You can always ride on my back.*

Soleil watched Elizabeth walk off into the dusk and followed her to the end of the property where the Adkins' farm stood. She waited on top of the hill and grazed and listened to the sounds of Elizabeth and Emily reliving the events of the day for Aunt Jenny and Uncle Phil.

"Emily," Aunt Jenny said during dinner, "we have a surprise for you."

"Honey, your aunt and I decided it's time for you to have your own horse—a mustang like Soleil. Elizabeth is going to help us choose one," said Uncle Phil.

"Then some day," added Elizabeth, "when Soleil lets me ride her with a saddle, we can go out on the trail together."

Emily was nearly speechless, it wasn't even her birthday. "No way!" she shouted happily and ran around the table to hug each and every one of them. "Now we really have to work on getting Soleil to wear that saddle!" she shouted happily.

"So now you think she *should* wear a saddle!" Elizabeth laughed and so did Emily.

As everyone enjoyed dinner and dessert, Soleil walked down the hill to her barn. She was tired. It had been a big day for her too.

There had been so many changes in her life since coming to live with Elizabeth. Changes that she never thought she'd be able to accept. She was no longer afraid of man, because she trusted Elizabeth. She loved her new home and found it easy to accept the new challenges one at a time.

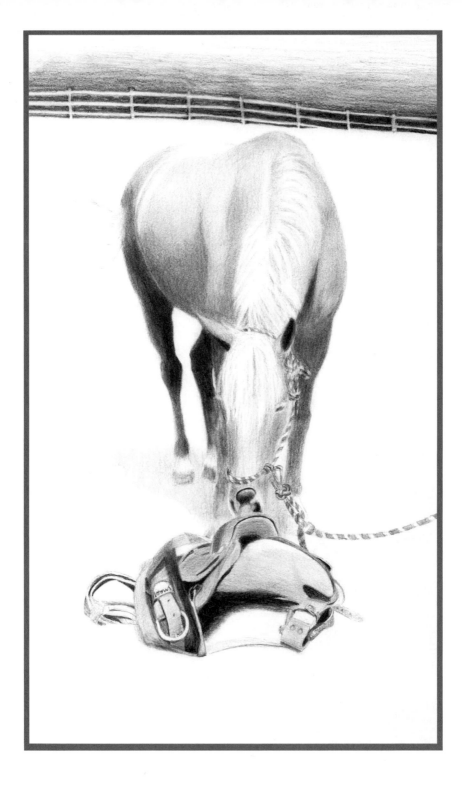

Chapter Ten

The Saddle

Elizabeth went down to the pasture the next morning on a mission. She had stayed up late that night after dinner reading books on horse training, trying to solve the saddle issue. She read that the girth was what usually bothered young horses, and that is was best to cinch it in stages to get the horse used to the way it felt.

Elizabeth went to the tack room and pulled out the saddle. Instead of putting it on Soleil, she threw it on the ground.

Soleil was curious and went over to inspect the saddle.

Elizabeth just stood there watching Soleil sniff the saddle. "There, girl, it's not going to hurt you," she said. At that moment, to Elizabeth's surprise, Soleil reared and stomped at the saddle and then ran up the hill. She turned around and looked at Elizabeth snorting as if to say, *It's not going to happen. No way!* Elizabeth just left the saddle on the ground. She walked over to Soleil and hoisted herself on top of her back.

Elizabeth rode Soleil around the pasture with nothing but a halter to guide her. After ten minutes had passed, she stopped Soleil near the saddle and slid off of her back. "It's okay, Soleil. You can just look at it today," Elizabeth said.

Soleil walked toward Elizabeth and dropped her nose to smell the saddle again. Soleil moved it with her nose and turned it over to smell the leather.

Elizabeth watched in silence. Soon Soleil started grazing.

Elizabeth got a treat for Soleil and sat it on top of the saddle. After Soleil took the treat off the saddle, Elizabeth said, "Enough for today." Then picked up the saddle and put it away.

Elizabeth did this every day for a week.

After three days, Soleil stood by the saddle and waited for a treat. "Good girl!" Elizabeth declared, giving her one. Every time Soleil saw Elizabeth with the saddle, she knew a treat would follow.

One day Emily was there when Elizabeth took the saddle to Soleil. This time Emily had the treat ready while Elizabeth brought out the saddle. Instead of putting the saddle on the ground, she put it on Soleil's back. Emily gave her a treat immediately. For a moment Soleil just stood there looking for more treats. Then Elizabeth reached underneath and pulled up the girth. As Soleil started to pin her ears back, Emily gave her a treat.

"That's right Emily, keep her occupied with food," Elizabeth said while tightening the cinch a little.

Elizabeth took Soleil's halter and walked her around the pasture, "It's not so bad is it girl?" she asked.

Elizabeth slowly tightened the cinch some more.

"That's it girl," she said finally hopping on.

Soleil didn't look happy about it, but she couldn't resist all of the treats.

Elizabeth let out a breath. It was a grand ending to the week. If Soleil kept doing this well, it wouldn't be long before they could go out on a real trail ride with some of their neighbors.

Emily and Elizabeth high-fived to their accomplishment.

"We just had to give the chow hound food!" Elizabeth declared. Together they laughed about how simple it had been.

Chapter Eleven

The Trail Ride

As summer came, yellow wildflowers blossomed in the field. Elizabeth made flower boxes on both sides of Soleil's barn; Emily thought it looked like something out of a fairytale.

Soleil stood inside the barn while Elizabeth and Emily adjusted her saddle. Whenever Elizabeth tightened the girth, she did it slowly. Soleil still pinned her ears but she was getting better about it.

"Today is going to be another special day," said Emily.

"Sure is! Soleil's first trail ride!" Elizabeth added.

Elizabeth had arranged to join her neighbors John and Joanne. They also had a small horse for Emily to ride until they found Emily her own horse. Elizabeth made her finishing touches and waved to her neighbors who were waiting on top of the hill.

John and Joanne had several older horses at their stable, good buddy horses for Soleil. Emily rode a little Paso Fino named Magic. Cheyenne wasn't going out today, but he watched them start on the trail. Soleil couldn't contain her own excitement *I can't wait to run free!* She thought, prancing at the gate.

"Ready to go?" John called out. Elizabeth gave him the okay sign. John was riding a big grey thoroughbred named Jake, and Joanne was riding a pretty bay quarter horse named Comet.

It was a new experience for Soleil, so she turned and looked at everything they passed— fallen trees, and gates—as she followed the other horses down the trail. It got a little spooky for her when the trail narrowed. "It's okay, girl. We'll take our time."

It seemed as though Soleil preferred the back because she didn't like the other horses behind her. She bucked a couple of times when Elizabeth asked her to trot.

Soon the trail opened up into a wide-open field. Soleil and Elizabeth cantered across it with the other horses. Elizabeth had to hold her back to keep her in control and said, "Soon girl, I'll let you run your heart out."

They slowed and came to a creek where the water was running swiftly. The other two horses plowed through, but Soleil pranced nervously back and forth while Elizabeth encouraged her to cross the creek. The other horses were around the bend and Soleil couldn't see them, she neighed for them but they were not paying attention to her.

She let out a squeal for the other horses. Elizabeth slowly persuaded her to go across. When she couldn't stand the isolation any longer, she plunged into the water bolting up the hill unseating Elizabeth in the process!

Out of the water and up the hill, she raced to catch up to the other horses, determined they wouldn't leave her behind. Elizabeth fell off Soleil quick and hard, knocking the breath out of her while Soleil raced onward. Soleil galloped so fast that Elizabeth barely caught a glimpse of her as she rounded the bend; Elizabeth's head hit the ground as she yelled "Soleil." Trying to get up was last thing she remembered.

Soleil realized that Elizabeth had fallen and had heard her call. She stopped suddenly when hearing Elizabeth's cry. She turned to the woman she trusted and loved that now laid unconscious on the ground. Love won over her fear and Soleil remembered how it felt when the herd left her behind. *Elizabeth, I will not leave you.* Soleil turned around in an instant and galloped back to where Elizabeth had fallen. Soleil nudged her *please be alright.* Soleil stood quietly while Elizabeth slowly came to her senses. Soleil overcame her own fears for the woman she loved. A stunned Elizabeth said, "You almost lost me girl, thank goodness for helmets."

John, Joanne, and Emily were up ahead with the other horses, Jake, Comet, and Magic. They were waiting for Elizabeth. They wondered why Soleil and Elizabeth had not caught up with them, and doubled back to see if everyone was okay. Rounding the bend Joanne saw that Soleil was standing over Elizabeth, while she was pulling herself up, clearly shaken. Soleil nickered to them, glad to be back with the group again. Joanne worryingly laughed at Elizabeth and Soleil. Elizabeth looked like she had seen a ghost. Her head pounded from the fall but otherwise she was okay.

"What a ride!" Elizabeth called out. She was very proud of Soleil for coming back for her. Elizabeth remounted a very quiet Soleil and said "Hey guys, I'm okay, I just took a tumble."

"There's a bridge up ahead," Joanne warned. "It backtracks over the stream we crossed."

"Okay, we'll be careful," Elizabeth answered, hoping Soleil would be a little calmer this time.

Soleil heard the sounds of the running water beneath her and balked with Elizabeth. She turned on her back legs and began to spin around. Elizabeth called out, "Whoa, girl!" She turned Soleil around so she could take a good look at the frightening bridge. Again the other horses walked across without incident, but it was the first bridge Soleil had ever seen.

Elizabeth kept turning her around, and Soleil was getting annoyed because she could not look at the bridge. Finally she gave in to Elizabeth, and Elizabeth stopped turning her. She now had Soleil's attention, and they started toward the bridge again. Soleil jigged back and forth at the beginning of the bridge, but she trusted Elizabeth, and her soft voice comforted her. "Come on girl, you can do it," she cooed. Soleil took one step onto the bridge. Nothing happened. Soleil took another step, and then another. Elizabeth said, "That's it girl, go on. There's nothing to be afraid of."

Soleil walked across, finally relaxed that the bridge wasn't going to swallow her up.

Emily waited for Elizabeth on the other side of the bridge. "She did really well," Emily said. "Don't you think so?"

"I sure do," Elizabeth said, relieved as they caught back up with John and Joanne and circled back around the trail on their way back home.

Soleil was relaxed now because she trusted Elizabeth and knew Elizabeth wouldn't take her somewhere dangerous. Soleil still kept her eyes open for anything abnormal, but being wild had taught her the difference between a breeze in the trees and a mountain lion. Her instincts taught her she was safe.

With her head set low, they continued the journey home. As they made their way to the narrow trail that led back to the farm, they picked up the pace a little and galloped in the soft sand leading home.

Elizabeth stopped Soleil on the final turn to make her walk back to the barn to cool off. Elizabeth was so happy that her laughter became infectious. Everyone appreciated how big an event this was for Soleil and Elizabeth. Soon everyone was laughing out loud.

Aunt Jenny and Uncle Phil were at the gate to meet them and to pick up Emily.

"Want to ride next weekend?" Elizabeth asked as she waved good-bye to John and Joanne and rubbed her sore head.

"You're on," Joanne confirmed, taking Magic's halter from Emily to lead him home.

"Wait till you see this!" Aunt Jenny yelled waving a copy of the *Rider's Gazette* as Elizabeth dismounted and walked toward them.

"It's finally published," added Uncle Phil. "You and Soleil are celebrities!" he teased. "Everyone wants to know more about the wild mustangs."

Elizabeth and Emily read the article and couldn't be happier.

"See how great you look, girl!" cried Emily, showing the photos to Soleil.

After all the excitement was over and they were alone, Elizabeth led Soleil to the barn and loosened the cinch and her saddle.

"Phew," Soleil loudly neighed, as if letting out a huge sigh of relief. She was still trying to get used to being all cinched up. Elizabeth laughed, then pulled her bridle off and went into the barn and came back with two of Soleil's favorite treats, oat muffins.

It was a big day for the two of them. Their first trail ride was a success, and the article would really bring attention to the cause of the mustangs. It was so important to Elizabeth. She wanted everyone to know how great the mustangs were. Elizabeth brushed Soleil down. Even if she had taken a tumble, it was a wonderful event. Elizabeth kissed Soleil's face and said, "You came back for me, girl, and looked out for me. Thank you." Tears of joy streamed from Elizabeth's eyes, and she held Soleil. Soleil looked up into Elizabeth's wet face and nickered back.

Chapter Twelve
The Talk

Since Aunt Jenny and Uncle Phil promised to let Emily get her own horse, they also wanted her to know how to ride properly and take care of her horse when she got it. They sent Emily to a summer horse camp for a few weeks and Elizabeth had not seen too much of her.

During that time, Elizabeth and Mrs. Adkins spoke quite a bit about Emily and getting her a horse of her own. Mr. and Mrs. Adkins and Elizabeth planned a big surprise for Emily when she finished camp.

On a summer afternoon while Elizabeth was down at the barn with Soleil, Emily came running down to tell Elizabeth all about horse camp.

Soleil nickered happily as if to say, *Where have you been?*

"I missed both of you, too," Emily said patting Soleil's neck and giving Elizabeth a big hug. Emily was bursting with information about camp. She had learned English riding while she was gone and was anxious to tell Elizabeth everything. While she did, Elizabeth got a soda out of the fridge in the barn and gave one to Emily. They let Soleil out into the pasture and walked behind her toward the oak tree.

Elizabeth rode western and was interested in all that Emily had learned at camp. It was a warm day, and the sun beat down on Elizabeth's face as she listened to Emily talk about horse camp from riding lessons, and how she had learned to post to the equipment she was learning to use.

It was obvious that Emily had really had fun at the horse camp.

"Well, it's about time you came home isn't it? Elizabeth asked her.

"I know. I didn't really want horse camp to end," Emily said. "I had so much fun."

Elizabeth eyes twinkled. "We have a surprise for you at home."

"Who has a surprise for me?" Emily stared at her.

"Soleil, your aunt, uncle, and me—that's who," Elizabeth said.

"What is it?" Emily asked pleadingly.

"It's a surprise!" Elizabeth baited her.

"Please tell me!" Emily squealed, hardly able to contain her excitement.

Elizabeth smiled at her and gave her another hug.

Soleil felt Emily's excitement and walked over to the two humans that she loved. She nuzzled Elizabeth's neck and put her head on her shoulder. Emily reached up and patted Soleil and smiled. "Well, okay. Aunt Jenny did say *I* could tell you," Elizabeth said before taking a deep breath to continue. "Emily, remember at dinner when your Aunt Jenny and Uncle Phil wanted to get you your own horse?"

Emily shook her head and said, "Yes!" At that moment it seemed that time stood still, you could have heard a pin drop.

"Well, we decided that we would lease you a horse for a while until we could find one that you liked."

"Really!" Emily shouted.

"I spoke to Joanne and John, and Magic will be your horse for a while," Elizabeth went on.

Emily was jumping up and down with joy.

She liked riding Magic and handled him well.

"But that's not the best part," Elizabeth added. Emily had reached up to Soleil's mane. Elizabeth took her hands, turned her around and stared into her eyes.

"I made a promise to Soleil a while ago. I promised her I would take her back to the high meadow where she was born."

"Are you really going to go there?" Emily asked.

"Yes, I am. I owe Soleil that much," Elizabeth answered. "If you want to, you could go with Soleil and me next summer. Elizabeth paused for a second. "And maybe you could look for a mustang of your own at the Bureau of Land Management's facility while we're out there." Emily's eyes went wide with excitement.

Then she hugged Elizabeth, "No way! Really?"

"A promise is a promise," Elizabeth said firmly. "Besides, the reporter who interviewed us about the wild mustangs wants to do a follow- up article on our trip west because the first article was so interesting to readers!"

Emily couldn't believe what she had heard

from Elizabeth. It was the happiest summer she could remember.

"But, Emily, for now you have to take care of Magic just like he was your own horse," Elizabeth told her. "And we can ride together with Soleil and Magic to practice for the trip," she added.

Soleil knew something big was going on. She raced and pranced back and forth across the pasture.

"I think that horse understands words," Elizabeth laughed. Emily smiled and looked at Soleil, "Yes Elizabeth. We both know she does."

The End

Conclusion

Soleil, *A Mustang's Story* is the first in a series of books about a wild mustang. For readers interested in learning more about the wild mustangs, or how to help them, sponsor, or adopt them, check the resources listed on the following page.

Lisa Holderby

Bureau of Land Management
Wild Horse and Burro Program
1-866-4MUSTANGS
www.wildhorseanburro.blm.gov

Front Range Equine Rescue
P.O. Box 8807 Pueblo, CO 81008
www.wildhorserescue.org

Black Hills Sanctuary
P.O Box 998
Hot Springs, SD 57747
1-800-252-6652
www.wildmustangs.com

Mustang Heritage Foundation
P.O. Box 703
Bertram, Texas 78605
512-355-3225
www.mustangheritagefoundation.org

United States Wild Horse & Burro Association
Hans F. Shull
63 Pingree Hill Rd. Derry, NH 03038
president@uswhba.org

Photo by Lisa Crosby

The author, Lisa Holderby, with Soleil.

Soleil drinking

Soleil in repose

Soleil